Erosion in the Grand Canyon has created many awesome and colorful rock formations. The rocks are as varied as the colors of the rainbow. Red, orange, purple, blue and even pink. At the bottom of the Grand Canyon is found the world's only "pink" rattlesnake. The snake has adapted itself to the canyon's pink color for its own protection. All rattlesnakes are dangerous. They slither along, then shake the rattles on the end of their tails before attacking. Rattlesnakes are sensitive to temperature, and in the summer usually come out only at night. In the winter the snakes move into caverns or rock crevices. Rattlesnakes swim readily and buoyantly across any lake or stream.

I AM AN ARO PUBLISHING
60 WORD BOOK
MY 60 WORDS ARE:

a	love	surprise
above	me	the
and	mule (mules)	their
are	my	there
around	old	they
but	on	think
Canyon	orange	this
duck	over	to
for	people	train
glide	pink	up
Grand	place	walls
great	rattle	want
green	rattlesnake	watch
ground	ride (rides)	water
hot	rocks	when
I	score	wiggle
in	skedaddle	will
is	slide	with
jump	Slitherfoot	won't
kick	Snake	yuk

GRAND CANYON CRITTERS

SLITHERFOOT

BY BOB REESE

ARO PUBLISHING

Old Grand Canyon
is the place I love,

With the Grand Canyon
walls up above.

The rocks are orange,
and green, and pink.
A great place for
Slitherfoot Snake, I think.

This place is
my rattlesnake slide.
A great place for
Slitherfoot Snake to glide.

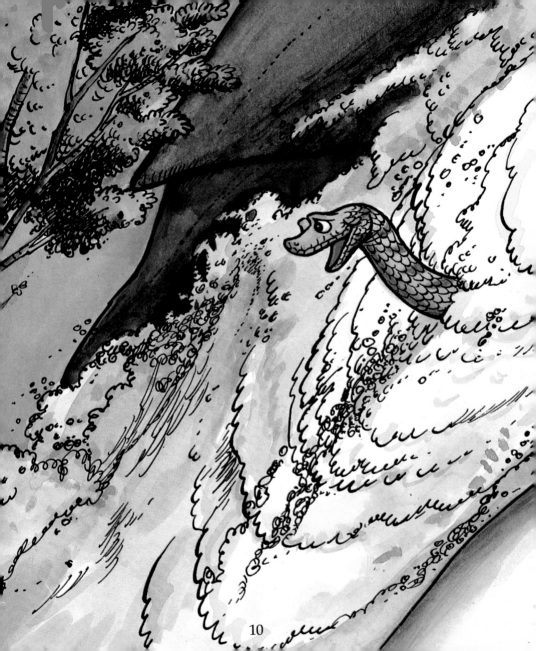

The water jumps the rocks
and is a slide.
I love the canyon
when the pink snake rides.

When the canyon rocks
are hot and yuk,

**Old Slitherfoot Snake
is a duck.**

Over there! Over there!
A mule train ride!
The people ride over
to slide on my slide.

I'll slide over there
and wiggle and rattle.
I'll scare the people
and watch them skedaddle.

**But the mules will kick
me on the ground,**

I won't scare the people
when the mules are around.

I'll wait for the people
to slide on my slide.

I'll jump in the water
and watch their surprise.

Old Grand Canyon
is the place I love.

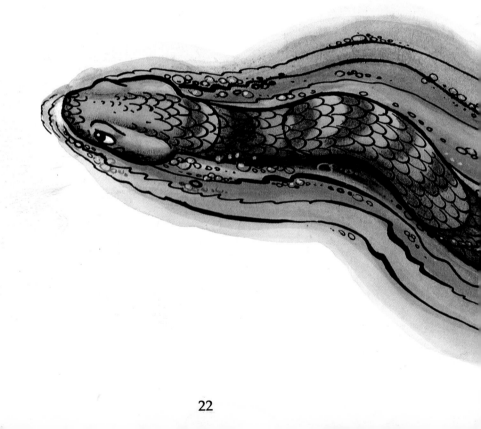

With the Grand Canyon
walls up above.